The author lives in Stockport, Cheshire. A grandmother and a retired nursery/infant and special needs teacher, she was inspired to write her own stories for young readers. She also hopes her stories will be useful to teachers and schools when introducing the minibeast theme.

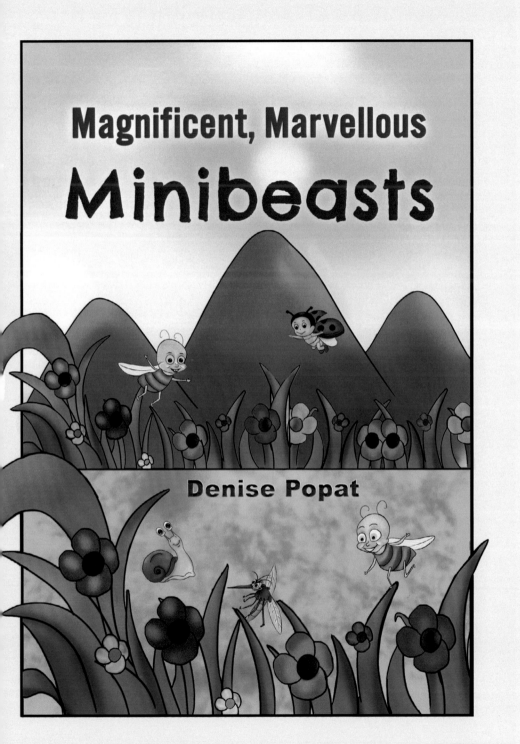

Magnificent, Marvellous
Minibeasts

Denise Popat

AUSTIN MACAULEY PUBLISHERS™

LONDON • CAMBRIDGE • NEW YORK • SHARJAH

Copyright © Denise Popat (2021)

A CIP catalogue record for this title is available from the British Library.

ISBN 9781398401648 (Paperback)
ISBN 9781398401655 (Hardback)
ISBN 9781398401662 (ePub e-book)

www.austinmacauley.com

First Published (2021)
Austin Macauley Publishers Ltd
25 Canada Square
Canary Wharf
London
E14 5LQ

I wish to dedicate this book to my granddaughter, Eva, and her little friend, Lizzie, who both loved listening to my stories and looking for minibeasts in the garden.

I would like to thank my two boys who encouraged me to write the stories, and to Darshana who helped proofread my stories.

Foreword

The aim behind my stories is to make a small collection of books which are useful in any special needs or infant classroom.

Having been a special needs teacher for many years, there are few books on the market which are sensory based, utilising our senses. We forget how important this is for any child, but more importantly to a special needs child who cannot experience his surroundings in the same way; often, we have to bring the experience to the child and a busy teacher needs to access resources quickly.

I used to adapt well-known stories to make them sensory based; this takes so much time and preparation. Perhaps we will be able to bring some of our outside environment inside for those who access with difficulty. The titles of the stories aim to help with the minibeast theme.

The Stories

Hi everyone, here is a short compilation of minibeast stories. Come and meet the gang, they are so excited to meet you. We have Freddy Frog, Sydney Snail, Sally Slippy Slug, Milly Molly Mosquito, Archie Ant, Belinda Buzz Bee, Gertie Grasshopper, Winnie Wiggle Worm, Willie Waspie and Siegfried Spider, just to name a few. The gang want to share their adventures with you, but most of all they want you to experience life from their perspective. If you like them, we can write more stories about the individual minibeasts.

FREDDIE FROG

Freddie Frog was the most amazing frog you ever did see; he wore a bright yellow hat and the most amazing green jacket. He was so proud of his green bare skin that he would often pose in the mirror, admiring himself.

Did you know? Frogs are amphibians and can live under water and also on land, which means they can't live away from water for too long but can breathe air through their nose, just like you and me. Some frogs feel slippery and slimy to touch because they are covered in a mucus coating. This helps them breathe through their skin. They use their skin to absorb oxygen when they are underwater.

Freddie's friends used to whisper conspiratorially, "There goes Freddie; what's he up to today, I wonder?" Freddie always managed to have an adventure every day, he never seemed to be able to keep himself out of mischief. Freddie Frog was actually an amazing jumper; do you know Freddie could jump 20 times his actual height? Wow, can you jump 20 times your own height?

Well, if you can't, don't worry, I think you can just try and jump like Freddy. Why don't you try...?

All of Freddie's friends thought he was such a kind and caring froggy; one would say, "A froggy you were proud to know!"

On this particular day, Freddie was about to embark on a gentle jump to the park and have a dip in the park pond; he thought he would catch a few flies, mosquitoes, moths and worms along the way, just to keep his tummy nice and full. To Freddie, all the things he ate would just be like cakes, biscuits and sweets to you. Freddie used to love listening to the children's excited chatter in the children's play area. He also loved to feel the gentle breeze on his face, listen to the rustling tree branches and smell and feel the cut green grass as he jumped along.

Freddie also enjoyed sunbathing, the feeling of the warm sunshine on his face, the tickling sensation of the scurrying ants beneath his feet and listening to the sounds of the birds chattering, chirping and calling as he drifted off to sleep.

Freddie stopped jumping when he found his favourite spot and thought to himself, *I will have my weekly sunbath and then shed and eat my skin.* Did you know frogs shed their skin once a week and eat it? Well, they do... but today Freddie was actually having a paddle at the pond's edge and a luxurious swim in the pond, just like you have when you go to the seaside; he loved the feel of the cold, soft and smooth water on his bare skin.

Freddie was laying on his back, relaxing, splashing and lapping up the water when he heard someone shouting, "Help, help, please, my baby tadpoles are hatching out of their frog spawn and are jumping all over the pond; I'm so frightened; I am going to lose some of my precious baby frogs."

Freddie leapt into action and shouted, "Don't worry, Mrs Frog, I will help you." Freddie shook the ripples of water off his back. He asked, "How many tadpoles do you have?"

Mrs Frog declared, "Ten!"

Freddie said, "I will catch them, fear not!"

Let's learn a few facts about tadpoles.

When the mummy frog lays the frog spawn, the daddy frog fertilises the sperms and the frog spawn hatch into tiny tadpoles.

The mummy frog lays her eggs on the plants. Hanging over the edge of the pond, the tadpoles hatch and they fall into the water. This is exactly what happened to mummy frog's babies.

Freddie caught the tiny tadpoles in his vocal sac; he splashed around the pond jumping behind pond bushes, algae and water lilies, ducking and diving until he counted ten tiny tadpoles. The tadpoles were weeping and wailing for their mummy. "We want our mummy," they shrieked and cried. They were so frightened, just like you are when you can't see your mummy. Freddie released the frogs to mummy frog in her little pond bush house.

Mummy frog scolded her tadpoles. She said, "Never ever, froggies, jump away from your mummy again!" You wouldn't jump away from your mummy, because frogs jump, and we run and walk, would you, children? It was lucky that Freddie was there to help. Freddie was so happy that he helped mummy frog and had done his good deed for the day.

With a large sigh of happiness, he went for another relaxing splash in the park pond and looked forward to his weekly sunbathe.

The End

BELINDA BUZZ BEE

Belinda Buzz Bee was always so busy.

Busy in the house, busy in the garden; she hardly ever found time to sit and talk with her friends as she was always so busy; *buzz buzz* buzzing around.

One day, Belinda Buzz Bee was feeling out of sorts. Everything had gone wrong on this particular morning; the flowers that needed pollinating had wilted and died due to a sudden heatwave and Belinda was tired, hot and cross in the heat. Her buzzing became a very loud buzzy sound to indicate to all her co-workers and friends how fed up she was. *Buzzzzzzzzzz buzzzzzzzz buzzzzz.*

Her friend, Walter Buzz Bee, said, "For goodness' sake, Belinda, sit down and take a rest! Your angry buzzing is making me cross and anxious. Also, stop beating your wings and come and eat some pollen and nectar from my beautiful bluebells; afterwards, we can eat the pollen and nectar from the apple tree at the bottom of the garden."

"Oh, alright," said Belinda, "if I must. But we can't rest for long as we have to strengthen our hive for queen buzz bee; she will not be amused if she knows we have been resting and we will be in so much trouble for not producing enough honey."

Buzzy bees eat the pollen and nectar from plants to help make honey. I am sure you all like honey on your toast at breakfast time.

Walt Buzz Bee was one of the male drones that mate with queen bees.

He said to Belinda, "Do you know when we are with queen buzz bee, we perform our wiggle dance in a figure–of–eight motion?"

"Really?" said Belinda.

"Oh come on, Belinda, you try it, please."

"Oh alright, Walt, if you insist. I'm not much good at dancing." Belinda and Walt both stood up and tried the wiggle dance to the sound of the swaying branches, which became alive and attempted to beat out a swing and sway rhythm. One, two, *buzz...* three, four, five, *buzz buzz...* six, seven, eight, *buzz buzz...*

Can you try it? Well, Belinda and Walt started to giggle and laugh; they had so much fun with their wiggle dance that Belinda soon forgot she was out of sorts.

All of a sudden, there was a very angry loud voice shouting, "What on earth do you think you are doing, Walter and Belinda. Get back to work this minute, you naughty bees! How am I going to run our hive if you two can't behave yourselves? You bad, bad bees."

Walt said, "Oh dear, so sorry, your majesty. But I was just trying to cheer up Belinda."

"Well, Walter, enough is enough. Join your drone this minute and fertilise my spawn as we need to protect our next generation of bees. As for you, Belinda, I'm hungry so go and make me some honey. Off you go back to your pollinating."

Walt and Belinda flapped their wings and flew away in disgrace, but if you looked closely, they both still had smiles on their faces. Happy *buzzzzzzz* bees.

The End

BERTIE BEETLE

I'm Bertie Beetle, my colour is black and I am about 25-mm long. I have two sets of beautiful wings; sometimes me and my beetle friends can be different colours — brown, green and blue — and can show off the beautiful metallic sheen on our beetle bodies. There are so many different types of beetles; I'm just the commoner gardener type that likes to live in the soil you find in your garden.

One day, my friend Cedric said, "Come on, let's go and explore the old garbage tip at the end of the road. I have been excited for ages to see what's in there."

"Okay," said Bertie. "Why not? We have got nothing else to do today. It's a wet, miserable day and there are too many clouds in the sky. I am fed up of going outside and getting drenched right through with rain."

"Oh, you are a misery today, Bertie. Why are you so out of sorts?"

"I am just fed up because of the weather, Cedric. All it has done these past few days is rain. I want to feel the sun on my face and feel the cool breeze running through my wings, Instead all I feel is wet right through, my shell—like exterior dripping under my tummy, *ugh!*"

"Well," said Cedric, "let's dance our way to the garbage tip. We can do the beetle bop, you can make knock knock and bang bang bang sounds as we amble along, all in rhythm to the beetle bop song!"

"Oh, alright," said Bertie.

"Look. *Knock,* one, two, three, *knock,* one, two, three and twirl around, flutter, *bang, bop,* one, two, one, two, *cha cha cha.* Now that's better!" said Cedric. "We will be at the garbage tip in no time and we can have great fun exploring and smelling what's inside there."

Bertie and Cedric climbed in the garbage tip and began to get very excited; they laughed loudly and started to excitedly chatter in beetle chatter — not sure how that sounds, children. Do you know? *Beet beet,* very fast maybe?

As they found bits of chopped-up wood, they both had a lovely time chewing the wood fibres. They also found dead flowers' petals, which they would love to eat and suck the nectar from. "This is so great," Cedric said, with Bertie completely forgetting what a miserable beetle he had been.

The beetles became more animated as they found old clothes. Beetles love to eat cotton and wool fibres. Bertie and Cedric rummaged a bit further into the tip and found old carpet. *"Mmmmmmm,* lovely wool fibres," said Bertie.

"Hey!" Bertie said. "Cedric, look what I have found. Some old cereal packets, cookies and chocolate, *whee!!!* Party time," Bertie said as they ducked, dived and delved further and further until they reached the bottom of the tip.

Today has turned out to be an amazing day, my friend. Well done for suggesting this. I have had a wonderful time finding so many lovely things to taste, smell and touch. My beetle feet have touched so many textures, can you remember? Wool, cotton, wood... there are probably so many different textures in the garbage tip not yet explored, children. I haven't even smelt the flowers, leaves or grass yet. Whoopi! Bye for now.

We are too busy for more conversation!!!

The End

GERTIE GRASSHOPPER

It was the most beautiful sunny day and Gertie Grasshopper was lounging fully stretched out on the grass, basking in the warmth of the sun.

Oh! Lovely sun, Gertie thought to herself. She felt warm and fuzzy all over her green grasshopper body. Grasshoppers can camouflage their bodies to match the colour of their surroundings. She stretched out her six legs and flapped her wings, enjoying the cool breeze which accompanied the brilliant yellow sunshine. Her antennae were twitching in excitement. *This is the life,* thought Gertie. *I am just going to let the world go by and enjoy a day of complete rest.* Famous last words, Gertie!!!

Gertie was woken up from her dreamy slumber by a loud *moo moo. Oh no*, thought Gertie. *I will have to move quickly before Mr Cow starts chewing the grass and me with it. Drat and bother! I was so happy relaxing.* Mr Cow came nearer and Gertie only just had time to jump up quickly before he was ready to chew her all up. Gertie jumped her highest jump ever: 25cm. *Wow!* thought Gertie. *It's a good thing I can jump so high; I thought I might have to fly!* Grasshoppers can fly too. Gertie moved as far away as possible from Mr Cow, but all her jumping made her hungry. *I will need to find some food soon,* thought Gertie.

Thank goodness I sharpened my pincers last night to tear the grass and leaves and to rip the heads off the farmer's cereal crops.

Gertie munched her way through all the lovely foods in the meadow until her poor stomach was half her body weight, full of plants and grass.

Gertie certainly needed a lie down again after all the food she had eaten. Gertie was soon to be disturbed again from her slumber. In the distance was the rumbling sound of thunder and lightning. Gertie was scared of the noise because she knew the flashes of lightning and thunder would give way to a torrential downpour. Sure enough, the little droplets of rain formed and fell on her face and body as the rain grew heavier and heavier and Gertie's ears started ringing with the loud claps of thunder.

Did you know grasshoppers have ears on their stomachs? Poor Gertie had a full stomach and ears that were vibrating!

Gertie flew away as quickly as she could into another meadow where there were plenty of bushes and trees. If that didn't protect her, she would find a field with tall grass or fly into the woods. Dear old Gertie Grasshopper, no peace in the meadow today!

The End

MILLY MOLLY MOSQUITO

Milly Molly Mosquito was a funny little insect. She spent a lot of her time pottering around the garden pollinating her favourite flowers and plants and playing little mosquito games with her mosquito friends.

They would play games like you do, such as 'mosquito tag' and 'follow the leader'. Most of the time, Milly Molly Mosquito was a very good little insect, but when she was vexed, she became very angry. You would not recognise this sweet little mosquito; her face would become all puckered and drawn and change colour; although mosquitos don't have teeth, she would bite ferociously at any other insects or humans passing by. Did you know, female mosquitoes bite three times their own weight in blood? Well, I didn't either until now!

Milly Molly Mosquito abhorred mean and horrible people, so when she saw them irritating other people, she would fly down and give then a short sharp bite. "Take that," she would say under her breath. She would then fly away as if nothing had happened.

The perks of being a mosquito, I guess! One day, Milly Molly Mosquito saw some grown men arguing in the street; they were fighting over a parking space. "I was there first," shouted the fat bald-headed man. "I'm not moving so what are you going to do about it?"

"Please, please," said the thin wiry bespectacled man. "I desperately need this car park space to visit my mother who is not well today. I may need to take her to the doctor's urgently."

"Hard luck, mate; my car is bigger than yours and I squeezed in here first, go away."

Milly Molly saw how horrible the fat balding man was so she flew down and bit him several times on the leg. "Ouch ouch," he screamed. He tried to swat poor old Milly Molly with his newspaper. He launched the newspaper several times in the air, lunging forward and missing Molly by the skin of her teeth, excuse the saying!!!

When Milly Molly attacked his bum in retaliation, his screeches were heard all the way down the street. He looked such a funny sight holding his leg and bum!!! People looked up and shook their heads because the men were causing a public disturbance. Milly Molly was enjoying the spectacle; she thought, *It serves you right, you horrible, selfish man.*

Well, the fat balding man got into his car, slammed the door with the most incredible thud, started up his car engine with loud revs and put his car into gear. Clunk click. "I'm going," he shouted. "Get out of my way, you stupid man." Milly Molly grinned with satisfaction; now the thin wiry bespectacled man could park his car in peace and go and visit his sick mother. When Milly Molly retold her story to her mum, her mum said, "Always be kind and considerate to people, and above all, be fair in life." Milly Molly thought, *I will listen to my mum's wise words.*

The End

WILLIE WASPIE

Hello, everybody. My name is Willie Waspie. Nobody really likes me or my family and friends; everybody is frightened that I might actually sting them, but did you know that it is only female wasps that can sting multiple times? Now I'm what you call a social wasp!

I spend most of my time in my drone building wasp nests to live in with my baby waspies and to help my other wasp friends build their homes too. I build my nest from wood fibres and I chew the fibre into pulp to shape the nest. I have two wings, a big tummy and narrow waist. On my head I have two antennae, biting and mouth parts. My legs are cylinder-shaped and I have a little bit of hair on my body. I like to eat the nectar from flowers, fruits, insects and spiders. Actually, I sound a bit funny, I agree! Perhaps check yourself out in the mirror too, as I kind of think you are funny-looking too. Really, children, I am a nice guy, honestly. I only get angry when people annoy me. I then fly around in circles and try to land on their hair and bodies. They often shriek and scream and try to swat me with a newspaper or a fly swatter, which annoys me even more. That's when I call my girlfriend Wilma, a queen wasp.

We all fly around in unison and irritate our prey for being so unkind to us. Wilma stings them for being so silly and annoying. Do you know if adults just left us alone, we wouldn't harm or hurt anybody! We are just trying to live our lives and work hard for our family. Wilma just wants to lay eggs for her baby wasps and I want to build a home for her.

We have a job to do and our role is to control parasites and pests. We control them for the farmer and for our ecosystem. Now I'm going to tell you a short story. One day, I was minding my own business building my nest when a group of men came by. They were naughty robbers and had obviously stolen goods from a shop.

The robbers were trying to hide the stolen items under the bushes where I was just building my nest in the lovely summer breeze surrounded by lots of bushes, foliage and greenery. I could hear lots of insect life scurrying in the undergrowth.

Dinner for later, I thought, licking my lips! The men were whispering conspiratorially and digging with their bare hands in the soil to hide and bury the things they had stolen. *What can I do to stop this?* I thought.

Willie had an idea. He contacted his drone and of course the beautiful Wilma wasp and some of her queen friends. At this point, Willie spotted the police who were approaching the lane very quietly, their footsteps hardly making any sound, looking for the robbers.

"Right waspies, action!" exclaimed Willie. Wilma and her friends started to fly around the robbers, attacking their hands and feet with wasp stings.

"Ouch! Ouch!" They shrieked, "Go away!" whilst jumping around and floundering in shock. The police caught up with the robbers and placed handcuffs around their wrists. Wilma and I were so happy that we had taught the robbers a very valuable lesson. Guess what it was, children?

The End

SALLY SLIPPY SLUG

Sally Slippy Slug was a sluggishly slow kind of sloppy slug. She would always try to wrangle herself out of situations and pretend she hadn't done anything wrong. I think you would say she was a sly and shifty sort of girl. Sally would do very naughty and unkind things to her friends and then say in a loud, haughty voice, "It wasn't me; it was..."

Well, I don't know what you think, everyone, but I think that's not very nice. Well, people can only get away for being so unkind for so long and then they are always taught a life lesson. Sally was about to discover this! Well, slugs are cold, wet and slimy creatures and if you touch them, they are all gooey and sticky because when they walk, they leave a slug trail of liquid crystal.

On this particular day, Sally was sliding and slithering along, munching some plants, worms and wild mushrooms along the way when a group of school children came along and tried to pick her up to take to their science lesson on minibeasts.

The ringleader of the group shouted to the others, "Come here, you lot; look at this slug, she's enormous!" Sally found herself being investigated in the hands of the ring leader. She said in excitement to the others, "Look at her tentacles, they are for seeing and smelling. Wow, can you see her teeth? Gosh, she has so many." Ugh!

Sally didn't like being a showpiece. She wanted to go back to eating plants, worms and mushrooms. Sally tried to bite her with her teeth so that she may leave her alone, but she didn't even feel the pain. She then tried to pull a trick and detach a piece of her body and escape. Do you know slugs can detach part of their bodies willingly and leave it behind? Sally then tried to make herself gooier and stickier so she would fall out of her hands but nothing was making this person let her go. Sally began to cry slug—like tears and wriggle furiously until in the end she successfully slipped from a height to the ground. Poor old Sally landed with a thud. She was so shocked, she couldn't move. All she wanted to do was lick her slug—like wounds. Along came some of Sally's friends.

They saw the school children run off. "Are you all right, Sally? We saw what was happening but we couldn't help you."

"I'm okay, thanks. A bit bruised and battered but I will live."

"Come on," they said. "We will help you home."

Sally was so shocked. "But I've been so mean to you. Why are you helping me?"

"Sally, we slugs have to stick together throughout life. Many people can be unkind, but it always takes the bigger person to be kind. Perhaps you will have time to reflect and think about this, Sally, and change your ways."

Sally hung her head in shame and said, "Please give me another chance. I will really try hard to mend my ways and not be mean anymore."

The End

SIEGFRIED SPIDER

Siegfried Spider was a friendly sort of spider. He had eight legs and came from the arachnid family; which means he's not an insect.

He just loved to scurry along, exploring different surfaces, textures and making silk, which he used to create his web.

The silk he creates is inside Siegfried's tummy; when he releases it, it comes out in a thread. Spiders use their web to catch little insects and small animals to eat.

They don't eat their prey because they have very small mouths, but they use a chemical from within their spider bodies to turn their prey into liquid and then suck them up! LOVELY.

Siegfried loved climbing into baths and up drain pipes, frightening people who were scared of him. He would laugh and giggle, thinking, *They are just so silly!*

Many of these people would scream and screech and become paralysed with fear. I know, readers, if you imagine there is a spider in your bath, what would you do?

Siegfried said, "Gosh, how ridiculous people can be. I am harmless. I'm just minding my own business, spinning my spider web and making silk."

Did you know, when you see cobwebs on your ceiling and walls, they are my abandoned cobwebs? Siegfried loved to play games on people who overreacted to his presence, so if you find lots of spider webs and cobwebs in your house, it's because Siegfried has made them to keep you busy.

Siegfried didn't like people who gave him a bath or flushed him down the toilet. He would curl himself up in a tight spider's ball until the tap was turned off or the flush finished.

Spiders love to live in people's houses.

You will always find in your house a Selina spider or a Siegfried spider.

They are all harmless, so don't worry or overreact. Spiders are eerie and creepy to touch, and they wriggle and try to tickle you as they move away; when they are free, they scurry across a room so fast.

Siegfried loved to climb on people's bodies and wait for a reaction, which was usually a loud pitched scream, and then scurry across the room as fast as his eight legs would carry him.

So, children, if you see a spider, he is harmless. He just wants to make his silk and eat his tea. He only plays games with you because you try to swat him with a newspaper and wash him away. Leave him alone and he will go away.

The End

LIZZIE LADYBIRD

Lizzie Ladybird was an absolutely astounding, beautiful ladybird. She had the loveliest ladybird face, black eyes and the sweetest smile. Her body was red and black with perfect black dots, seven in all, placed in perfect symmetry. Her body was dome-shaped, and she had six graceful, short legs. Everybody in the minibeast world said, "There goes the beautiful Lizzie. She is so proud and haughty." Not only did the minibeasts admire Lizzie, so did the local farmer, because Lizzie and her ladybird family ate his plant-eating pests and because the seven spot ladybirds are meant to indicate 'good luck' to all who cross their paths.

Ladybirds flutter around and walk through grassland where there is plenty of foliage, leaves and vegetation. Lizzie strutted past the minibeasts on her way to visit some ladybird friends who were working busily near the local river.

43

It was a beautiful sunny day, the birds were singing in the trees and the tree branches were swishing and swaying in the cool breeze. Lizzie stopped on her journey to graze hungrily on a few aphids. Aphids are little bugs which eat the sap from plant life. As Lizzie was eating, a small frog jumped by and tried to pounce upon poor Lizzie's back. He was attracted by her lovely bright colours. *Aha!* thought Lizzie. *I will release my secretion of yellow fluid from my back legs; take that, you naughty frog; it tastes disgusting, so leave me alone!*

Well, the frog was somewhat startled by this; he jumped up and started to hop away as quickly as his frog legs would carry him.

Lizzie regained her composure and continued to graze when a green grassy grasshopper came by. *Not again,* thought Lizzie. *Maybe it will go away.* But the grasshopper jumped nearer and nearer.

This time Lizzie played dead because this is another defence tactic that ladybirds use. The grass hopper jumped away in disgust. No live prey to eat!

By this point, Lizzie thought, I *better be on my way and find the river before any other predators try to eat me.* Lizzie thought to herself, *You can't even take a nice stroll to the river without being attacked!!! What's the minibeast world coming to? I really don't know.*

At last Lizzie arrived. Her ladybird friends were so happy to see her. They shouted, "Hi Lizzie! We are so pleased you have come. We have been busily working in our ladybird colony."

Her friend Leonie said, "Lizzie, I'm so pleased to tell you that I have some exciting news. I'm going to have some babies; come and see!"

Leonie took Lizzie to a tree sapling and showed her all her clusters of larvae on the leaf. The babies would feed off the aphids in the leaves. Lizzie was so happy for Leonie. She said, "Come on, we deserve a little paddle and dip in the river. Let's enjoy the lovely warm sunshine basking on our bodies with a glass of chilled water in our hands, have our ladybird chit chat and catch up with the ladybird news."

The End

ARCHIE ANT

Archie was a wonderful specimen of an ant. Wherever he went, he would scurry along, preen and pose knowing he had a marvellous reflection. Archie had grown into a fine figure of an ant and he knew it! Archie was very conceited, as you can imagine!

He thought he knew everything he needed to know about ant life. Archie was the eldest of three siblings and he bossed his sister and brother around terribly.

Actually, he was a very naughty ant, between you and me! His mum and dad had to shout at Archie every single day because he just wouldn't behave himself.

To be honest, Archie didn't even try. One day, Archie took a step too far and although he didn't know it, he was in for the biggest shock of his life.

His siblings were about to teach Archie a lesson, they were so fed up of him. Archie had the habit of eating their food before they even had a chance to catch, reach or eat it. They would often go hungry and have nothing to eat until teatime, when their mum made sure all their food was divided equally. Archie was just about to pinch their food at breakfast time when his siblings secretly put salt in his dish. Ants love food with sugar and nectar, but not salt, ugh!

"Ugh! Cough, splutter!" said Archie when he got a mouthful of salt. "Disgusting!" So Archie walked away hungry. The next meal at lunch time, the siblings did the same. Archie was so hungry by this point, in disgust he rushed off to see if he could find some of his own food. The siblings laughed so much, their sides hurt. "Serves Archie right, we don't care," they said. "We are always hungry because he's so very selfish and conceited."

The next game they played on poor Archie was to cover up all the mirrors in the house so Archie couldn't see himself.

They painted them black so all Archie could see was a black blob.

Archie was mortified. He shouted, "I have lost my beautiful shape and I have become so ugly and fat." He began to cry, stamp and shout. "What is happening to me?" The crocodile tears began to fall down his face and he rubbed and sniffed his nose, muttering to himself, "Why is everyone being so unkind to me??? It's just not fair."

The siblings had still not finished with Archie! All the years of hurt and unkindness from Archie had built up, so they then planned to find the largest drum they could bang and blast.

Poor Archie was about to experience some very loud vibrations. Archie jumped up in fright and screamed loudly, "Ahhhhhh!" He was frantic. Ants don't have ears but listen through vibrations and their antennae.

His siblings then tricked Archie to lift an apple filled with soya sauce. Archie thought he was going to eat a lovely sweet juicy apple but fell for their trap because, being Archie and very conceited, Archie knew he was a strong ant and capable of lifting things 20 times his body weight. He pulled and pulled at the apple, anticipating a nice juicy treat, only to struggle to lift the apple and then taste a mouthful of soya sauce, *ugh!!!* Archie said, "I'm so hungry!"

The apple was actually 40 times his own weight. Archie stumbled and fell back onto the ground. He'd still not had anything to eat, poor Archie! Archie began to realise how awful he had been to his siblings. He offered to fight their future battles with other ants, look for their food and help build with the other ants their share of building the new ant colony. The lesson: always be kind to your siblings!

The End

WINNIE WIGGLE WORM

Winnie Wiggle Worm was slithering, sliding and ambling along the garden path at a wiggle-worm-like pace when she heard the excited chatter of children's voices. Winnie loved to hear the children play and listen to the games they invented. She would listen and imitate their ideas with her wiggle worm friends. Today the children were playing an inventive game called 'Mr Monster Crunch'. Mr Monster Crunch was an imaginary monster; when the children played their game of hide-and-seek, instead of saying, "YOU ARE OUT," when they were found and caught, he gobbled them all up. "Well, I never," you say. Well, do remember he was only an imaginary character.

He was a funny-looking monster with brown shaggy hair, enormous black blue eyes, a large body, small hands and feet; his nose was wet and felt very cold to touch; he had large white teeth that stuck out at irregular angles all over his large mouth. *Oh dear!* thought Winnie Wiggle Worm. *This might be a difficult game to play with my wiggle worm friends, but we can always try. Maybe Wilbur Wiggle Worm would be the perfect choice as he is the biggest worm in our group, and he is definitely the ugliest.* Wilbur was always teasing them, laughing and telling wiggly worm jokes. "What did the worm say to...?" He was a good friend of Winnie's so she was sure he would play.

We will have to make him look more like a monster, I think! The children always had different game ideas every day. There were shrieks and cries of laughter as Mr Monster Crunch came to find them; he would give a warning shout, *"Grhhhhhhhhh grhhhhhhh,* I'm coming, my lovelies," and then he would shout in his gravelly, booming voice, "I'm coming, ready or not. One, two, three, four, five, six, seven, eight, nine, ten, *mmmm,* ha ha, it's dinner time for me! I have been dreaming all night about how I am going to enjoy these lovely, wriggling, squirming children; how perfect. Lovely!"

As Mr Monster Crunch was getting near the hiding children, he would huff, puff and blow out lots of air and his nostrils would flare wide open. The air he blew could lift the children in the air, so he would then catch them in his outstretched arms, tickle their arms and legs and gobble them all up!!!

Not really; remember, it's only an imaginary game? Winnie tried to imagine Wilbur throwing the wiggly worms in the air and catching their wriggling bodies — not an easy task for a wiggly worm!!! Wilbur also had a very squeaky high-pitched voice, so when he counted one, two, three, four, five, six, seven, eight, nine, ten and shouted, "Coming, ready or not," it sounded like an off-key violin! Wilbur's worm body was so smooth, soft and silky, he slithered so quickly through the undergrowth that there was no comparison to the noise Mr Monster Crunch made as he ran through the under growth like a baby elephant: *thud thud thud, stamp stamp,* knocking tree branches back, kicking stones and pebbles and making gigantic footsteps that caused the grass to swish and sway with a whoosh of air that went by saying, "Can you hear him? He's coming!"

Well, the wiggle worms had a wonderful time that afternoon emulating Mr Monster Crunch game. They all took it in turns but Wilbur was the best because his squeaky voice made them giggle and laugh and gave them an inkling of when he was coming. Winnie thought she was the best at the game because she slithered, slathered and ambled along so quietly that the other wiggly worms were taken by surprise. She was able to tunnel very deeply in the soil and other wiggle worms found it difficult to find her. Well done, Winnie Wiggle Worm! I wonder what games the children will play tomorrow! Perhaps they will do a wiggle worm dance...

The End

Earthworm facts: did you know, worms can eat anything as long as it's dead, but they mainly eat leaves and soil as it provides potassium and nutrients for them. Worms have no lungs and breathe through their skin. Worms also have no eyes, arms or legs.

Worms live where they can find food, moisture and oxygen. Worms tunnel deeply in the soil, where they make a slime trail which contains nitrogen; this gives nitrogen to plants.

Did you know, baby worms hatch from cocoons smaller than a grain of rice. both male and female worms produce eggs and sperm.

SYDNEY SNAIL

Sydney Snail was a rather large snail who lived in the bottom of Eva's garden. Eva was a very inquisitive child of three years, with brown hair and beautiful brown eyes. She was so sweet and gentle by nature that all the minibeasts in the garden loved her. Eva's favourite minibeast in the whole wide world was one of the snails; she would call him Sydney.

"Sydney, I'm here," shouted Eva in her perfectly sweet, little voice. "Where are you?" Sydney always popped his head out of his house shell and rushed over to see Eva. Well, that is, if a snail can rush! Let's say as fast as he could leave his little snail trail and as fast as his little snail legs would carry him. Eva said, "I have brought you some lovely flowers and leaves to eat today; and Sydney, I have found you a nice muddy puddle of water to drink from." Sydney was so happy as he'd been feeling rather peckish and thirsty. Eva said to Sydney, "Do you know you are rather strange–looking? You have such a large shell and funny storks sticking out on your head."

Sydney just looked at Eva and said, "Hahaha, Eva, you look pretty funny to me also. Do you know what? My teeth are sharper than yours, Eva, so I can rip my food into small and tiny pieces and that's what I am about the do with the lovely lunch you have brought me."

Eva smiled at Sydney and said, "Look at my beautiful white baby teeth. My Mummy tells me I will get new teeth when I am older."

"Hmmmm," said Sydney, continuing to eat his lunch, lifting his head to acknowledge Eva's incessant chatter.

Eva said to Sydney, "Will you play with me? I've no friends to play with me today and I'm so fed up."

"What do you want to play, Eva?" said Sydney. "How about snail trails and Eva trails? I will leave my mucus snail trail all around the garden and you can leave your Eva trail!" What do you think Eva's trail might be? Think of three-year-olds leaving their toys all over the floor or the garden. Eva ran off and started playing with her toys for a few minutes and then discarding them, leaving a trail all over the grass and even onto the garden path! Eva didn't leave her trail in the flower borders or bushes because there were lots of rose bushes which pricked her little arms and legs.

Sydney was having a lovely time in the bushes eating all the flower heads and stems. *Ha,* thought Sydney, *I can amuse myself whilst Eva tires herself running round the garden playing.*

Sydney snuggled down to have forty winks and lazily chew on a stem of flowers. Eva ran around the garden shouting, "Sydney Snail where are you?" and as little children do, she continued to play for five minutes with one toy and then move on to the next leaving her little toy trail. Sydney opened one eye, oblivious to Eva's chatter and dreamed peacefully on until there was a piercing shrill scream and a cry for help. Poor little Eva had caught her foot in a prickly bush. Tears were streaming down Eva's face. Sydney felt very sad and helpless for one moment until he had the most incredible, amazing idea.

He said, "Hang on, little Eva, I'm going to call on all my snail friends to eat the stems of the bush, so the bush will collapse where your foot is trapped." Sydney shouted in snail language to all his snail friends. They all came as quickly as snails can and devoured the bush where Eva's foot was trapped. At last, Eva was set free. She was so relieved as she rubbed her foot with her hand.

Eva shouted, "Sydney, I love you and will always look after you. Thank you so much, my lovely snail friend." Sydney Snail was so happy he had helped his little friend Eva. It was a great accolade for a common garden snail to have achieved, especially amongst his snail friends.

The End